KING ROLLO'S
Christmas

To Jill, Euan, Peter and the
Watermill Theatre

A Red Fox Book

Published by Random Century Children's Books
20 Vauxhall Bridge Road, London SW1V 2SA

A division of the Random Century Group
London Melbourne Sydney Auckland
Johannesburg and agencies throughout the world

First published by Andersen Press Ltd 1990

Red Fox edition 1992

Printed in Hong Kong

ISBN 0 09 973980 1

David McKee
KING ROLLO'S
Christmas

RED FOX

"Only two days to Christmas," said King Rollo.

"Oh dear," said the Magician. "Something terrible has happened. Someone has cut off Santa's beard."
"He can wear a pretend one," laughed King Rollo.

"Santa is Santa, beard or no beard," said Queen Gwen.

"But the beard is magic," said the Magician.

"That's how Santa visits everyone in one night."

"Without the beard...."

"No presents for anyone," finished King Rollo.

"You have to do something, Magician,"
said King Rollo.
"Make a spell so the beard grows quickly."

"It is not easy because it's a magic
beard," said the Magician.

"Have you found a way to make Santa's beard grow?" King Rollo asked a little later.

"Well there is a spell," said the Magician. "I need that liquid and this powder, then three hairs from a growing beard."

"I have those," said King Rollo.

"Three white hairs," said the Magician.

"Hamlet has those," said Queen Gwen.

"And some of the beard taken from Santa," said the Magician.

"I know the beard was cut by Darl," said the Magician. "He lives in Dark Dale woods. It could be dangerous. We shall have to be careful."

"What do you mean – 'WE'?" said Cook.

"We shall all have to go," said the Magician. "The things have to be kept separate. I'll carry the liquid. You, Cook, can carry the powder."

"I'll carry my beard," said King Rollo.
"And Hamlet will carry the white hairs."

"And I can carry Santa's beard," said Queen Gwen.

"If and when we get it," said the Magician.

"We *have* to get it," said King Rollo. "Or no Christmas presents for anyone."

"Anyway it will be cold, especially when we get to Santa," said Cook. "So get your warm things."

When they were all dressed warmly the Magician said: "If we're all ready, we'll go." They stood in a circle and held hands. The Magician's hat pointed at each of them and then there was a...

The next instant they were standing among trees. "Is this Dark Dale woods?" asked King Rollo.
"Yes," said the Magician. "Magic won't take us through here – we have to go on foot.
"It is very dark," said Queen Gwen.

"Stay close and we'll be all right," said the Magician.
"Be all right," said King Rollo. "Why shouldn't we be all right?"

"Well," said the Magician. "We might have problems with Wicked Witch Wiolet and her Woozy Web."

"Woozy Web?" the others said together. "What's a Woozy Web?"

"This is," cackled a voice and a sticky net fell out of the trees and trapped them all.

A witch appeared from behind a tree. "That is the Woozy Web," she said.

"And I am the Wery Wonderful Wiolet," she added, "and I've caught you."

"Oh dear," said Cook.

"Oh dear," said the Magician.

"Oh dear," said Queen Gwen.

Hamlet said nothing.

So King Rollo said, "Oh dear, oh dear."

"Oh dear, oh dear, oh dear," laughed Wiolet.

"I'm stuck, it's glue," said King Rollo. "That's the wooze," chuckled Wiolet.

"Please let us go," said Queen Gwen. "We have to get to Santa or there won't be any Christmas presents."

"No presents? Whoopee!" said Wiolet. "See you tomorrow!" And off she went cackling merrily.

"This is terrible," said King Rollo as they tried to get free.

"Do something, Magician," he added.

"I can't," said the Magician. "My hat has come off and my hands are stuck."

"Quiet," said King Rollo as they heard someone singing. "Wiolet is coming back."

"It sounds too nice for her," said Queen Gwen.

The singing came closer and a man appeared. "Hello," he said. "Are you happy there? Or shall I set you free?"

"Free please," they answered. "Ha ha, what fun," said the man and he started squirting with a water pistol.

"Stop it," said Queen Gwen.
"I thought you wanted to be free," said the man.
"It's not water, you know."

"The web's vanishing," said King Rollo.

By the time they were all free the man was already leaving.
"Be careful where you go," he said.

Then he added, "You shouldn't be here really."

"He's right," said Cook. "I hope we don't have any more nasty adventures."

"Now what, Magician?" asked King Rollo. "On to find Darl's tower of course," said the Magician. "Come on."

After a long walk they came to a clearing. On the other side was a tower. "Darl's tower," said the Magician. "Be very careful."

Near the tower they stopped and peeped from behind some rocks. "I'd like to know what kind of person Darl is before we go any closer," said the Magician.

Just then they heard singing. "The man who saved us from Wiolet," said King Rollo. "Perhaps he can help us again."

Sure enough the same man appeared. "Hello," he said. "Are you lost?"

"We are looking for Darl," said King Rollo, "but we don't know what he looks like."

"Come on in," said the man. "I'll introduce you. Don't be frightened, just tell me your names."

"I'm King Rollo," said King Rollo. "This is Queen Gwen, Cook, the Magician and Hamlet the Cat."

"And I'm Darl," laughed the man.

"You?" said King Rollo. "You're the one who cut Santa's beard?"

"The very same," laughed Darl. "Santa was asleep so I snipped off his beard. What a joke!"

"A joke," gasped King Rollo. "Don't you know there may not be any Christmas presents because of you?"

"What?" gasped Darl.

"The beard is the magic that lets Santa travel so fast," said Queen Gwen.

Darl went pale. "What can we do?" he said.

"Do you have any of the beard you cut off?" asked the Magician.

"Yes, it's here. I kept it as a souvenir," said Darl.

"I'll take that," said
Queen Gwen.

"Will we be in time?"
asked King Rollo.

"Yes, with luck," said
the Magician. "Tomorrow
is Christmas Eve."

"It's late," said Darl. "Sleep here
and start early in the morning.

"Lucky you have plenty of beds,"
said King Rollo.
"I'll be careful what tricks I play
in future," said Darl.

In the morning they went to the top of the tower. "Hold hands in a circle again I suppose," sighed Cook. The Magician's hat did its work.

"Where are we?" asked King Rollo a moment later.
"Santa's palace," said the Magician "and here come his gnomes."

They were taken to Santa who was looking sadly in the mirror. "Don't worry Santa, we can make it grow," said King Rollo.

"We hope," muttered the Magician, and explained everything to Santa.

Cook put the powder in a bowl.

Queen Gwen added the pieces of beard that Darl had given them.

Three hairs from King Rollo's beard went in.

Then three white hairs from Hamlet.

Finally the Magician added the liquid.

The mixture was rubbed on Santa's face.

After that they waited for the beard to grow.

By mid-day it had started to grow.

At tea-time Santa said, "It will be grown by the time we want to leave."

"WE?" said Cook.

"I'll take you home on the way," said Santa.

At midnight they were ready to go and the beard was back to normal.

"Thanks to you it's Christmas as usual," laughed Santa as they started their journey across the night sky. That was almost all they remembered of the journey.

The next morning King Rollo was happy to wake up in his own bed.

When they opened their presents the Magician said, "Good old Santa."

"Good old Magician as well," said Queen Gwen.

"Let's say good old all of us," smiled King Rollo. "Happy Christmas, everyone."

Some bestselling Red Fox picture books

THE BIG ALFIE AND ANNIE ROSE STORYBOOK
by Shirley Hughes
OLD BEAR
by Jane Hissey
JOHN PATRICK NORMAN MCHENNESSY –
THE BOY WHO WAS ALWAYS LATE
by John Burningham
I WANT A CAT
by Tony Ross
NOT NOW, BERNARD
by David McKee
THE STORY OF HORRIBLE HILDA AND HENRY
by Emma Chichester Clark
THE SAND HORSE
by Michael Foreman and Ann Turnbull
BAD BORIS GOES TO SCHOOL
by Susie Jenkin-Pearce
MRS PEPPERPOT AND THE BILBERRIES
by Alf Prøysen
BAD MOOD BEAR
by John Richardson
WHEN SHEEP CANNOT SLEEP
by Satoshi Kitamura
THE LAST DODO
by Ann and Reg Cartwright
IF AT FIRST YOU DO NOT SEE
by Ruth Brown
THE MONSTER BED
by Jeanne Willis and Susan Varley
DR XARGLE'S BOOK OF EARTHLETS
by Jeanne Willis and Tony Ross
JAKE
by Deborah King